MARIE-LOUISE FITZPATRICK is an award-winning
Irish author and illustrator, whose books *Izzy and Skunk*
and *You, Me and the Big Blue Sea* have both won the
Bisto Book of the Year Award. Her warm and distinctive
style has attracted fans from all over the world.
Beth, the heroine of *Silly Baby*, is based on Marie-Louise's
own niece. You can read more about Beth's adventures in
Silly Mummy, Silly Daddy, and *Silly School*, both published
by Frances Lincoln Children's Books.

For Michael, all my love – *M-L.F.*

JANETTA OTTER-BARRY BOOKS

First published in Great Britain and in the USA in 2010
by Frances Lincoln Children's Books, 4 Torriano Mews, Torriano Avenue,
London NW5 2RZ

www.franceslincoln.com

First paperback edition published in Great Britain in 2010 and in the USA in 2012

British Library Cataloguing in Publication Data available on request

The illustrations in this book are in gouache

ISBN: 978-1-84780-123-4

Printed in Bangkok, Thailand by Kyodo Nation Printing Services in November 2009

1 3 5 7 9 8 6 4 2

Silly Baby

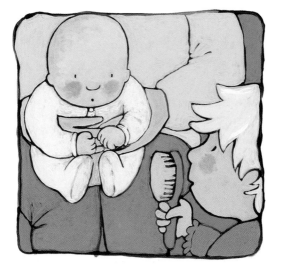

Marie-Louise Fitzpatrick

FRANCES LINCOLN
CHILDREN'S BOOKS

There's a new baby.

It's a boy.

He can't walk.

He can't talk.

He's got no hair.

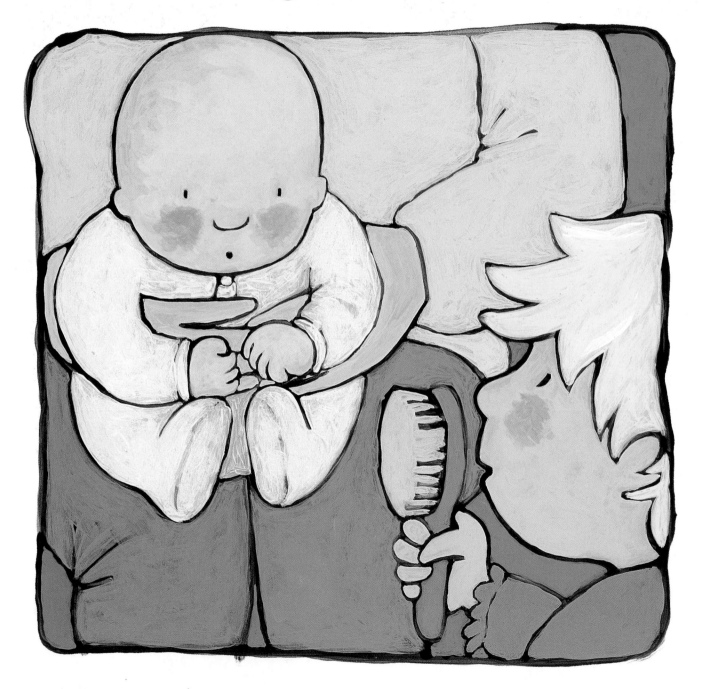

Silly baby!

He cries.

He sleeps.

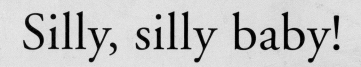

Silly, silly baby!

Granny has the silly baby.

Beth has the silly baby.

He smiles.

He's soft.

He's a little bit silly...

...but he's *my baby brother.*

MORE PAPERBACKS FROM
FRANCES LINCOLN CHILDREN'S BOOKS

Silly Mummy, Silly Daddy
Marie-Louise Fitzpatrick

Beth is VERY cross today and will not smile – not even
a little bit! The whole family tries to put her in
a sunny mood but they are all just SILLY!
Can clever big sister save the day?

Silly School
Marie-Louise Fitzpatrick

Beth doesn't want to go to silly school!
She doesn't want to go for storytime, or painting,
or singing. So what does she want to do?

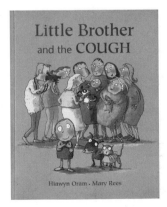

Little Brother and the Cough
Hiawyn Oram
Illustrated by Mary Rees

When a new baby brother arrives in the family, it's not
always easy. In this case it leads to a Cough, a very Bad Cough,
a very very VERY Bad Cough!
Poor big sister. No one seems to notice how she feels . . .
until at last the Cough becomes desperate, and people listen to it,
and soothe it. And suddenly a little girl finds that she can talk
to her baby brother, after all.

Frances Lincoln titles are available from all good bookshops.
You can also buy books and find out more about your favourite titles,
authors and illustrators on our website: www.franceslincoln.com